The Colony of Georgia

A Primary Source History

The Rosen Publishing Group

PowerKids Press™
PRIMARY SOURCE

Melody S. Mis

To Georgians Mike & Claudia and Ron & Ellen

Published in 2007 by The Rosen Publishing Group, Inc.
29 East 21st Street, New York, NY 10010

Copyright © 2007 by The Rosen Publishing Group, Inc.

First Edition

Editor: Jennifer Way
Book Design: Ginny Chu
Layout Design: Julio Gil
Photo Researcher: Marty Levick

Photo Credits: Cover and title page, p. 14 (inset) © North Wind Picture Archives; p. 4 © Private Collection, Ken Welsh/Bridgeman Art Library; p. 4 (inset) The New York Public Library/Art Resource, NY; p. 6 © Courtesy of the Trustees of Sir John Sloane's Museum, London/Bridgeman Art Library; p. 6 (inset) Georgia State Archives; pp. 8, 12 Ed Jackson; pp. 8 (inset), 16 (inset), 18 (inset) Courtesy of the Georgia Historical Society; p. 10 © Private Collection/Bridgeman Art Library; p. 10 (inset) © North Wind Picture Archives/Nancy Carter; p. 12 (inset) Library of Congress, General Collections; p. 14 © Time Life Pictures/Getty Images; pp. 16, 18 © Getty Images; p. 20 Library of Congress Map Division; p. 20 (inset) Independence National Historical Park.

Library of Congress Cataloging-in-Publication Data

Mis, Melody S.
   The colony of Georgia : a primary source history / Melody S. Mis.
      p. cm. — (The primary source library of the thirteen colonies and the Lost Colony)
   Includes index.
   ISBN 1-4042-3433-0 (library binding)
   1. Georgia—History—Colonial period, ca. 1600–1775—Juvenile literature. 2. Georgia—History—1775–1865—Juvenile literature. 3. Georgia—History—Colonial period, ca. 1600–1775—Sources—Juvenile literature. 4. Georgia—History—1775–1865—Sources—Juvenile literature. I. Title. II. Series.
   F289.M57 2007
   975.8'02—dc22

                              2005025625

Manufactured in the United States of America

Contents

Savannah

CARTE
DE LA PARTIE SUD
DES ETATS UNIS
DE
L'AMERIQUE SEPTENTRIONALE.
Par M. Bonne Ingénieur Hydrographe
de la Marine.

This eighteenth-century map shows part of the southeast Atlantic coast of North America. In the 1500s, European explorers, such as Hernando de Soto, visited this area, part of which would become Georgia. Inset: Spanish explorer Hernando de Soto lived from about 1500 until 1542.

Discovering Georgia

The first European known to have come to Georgia was the Spanish **explorer** Hernando de Soto. He landed in Georgia in 1540 to search for gold. Although de Soto did not find gold, he claimed land for Spain. The Spanish did not colonize Georgia at this time. They were more interested in finding gold and other riches to ship back to Spain. The Spanish did not want other Europeans to settle on the land they had claimed, however.

To prevent other Europeans from settling in North America, Spain built military outposts, called forts, along the coast. In 1566, the Spanish built a fort on Saint Catherines Island in Georgia. Because Spain controlled the southeast Atlantic coast, Georgia remained unsettled by Europeans from 1564 until 1733.

From Georgia's Charter

"Whereas we are credibly informed, that many of our poor subjects are . . . reduced to great necessity. . . . [T]hey would be glad to settle in any of our provinces in America where by cultivating the lands, at present waste and desolate, they might not only gain a comfortable subsistence for themselves and families, but also strengthen our colonies and increase the trade, navigation and wealth of these our realms."

The opening part of Georgia's charter says that the trustees know that there are many poor British people who would be happy to settle in an American colony and start a new life. Such a colony would in return be good for Britain because it would make money for Britain and also strengthen the country's claims in North America.

During the eighteenth century, British people who could not pay back money they owed to others were sent to debtor's prisons like the one shown here. James Oglethorpe wanted to help debtors begin new lives in the Georgia colony. Inset: Georgia's 1732 charter granted control of the colony to the trustees for 21 years, after which it would become a royal colony.

Oglethorpe's Grand Plan

James Oglethorpe was a member of Parliament, England's government. In 1732, he had an idea for a way to help British **debtors**. At that time the British jailed debtors. Oglethorpe made plans with 20 men, who were called the Georgia Trustees. They asked George II, king of Britain, to grant land to the trustees. They would establish a colony in America where Britain could send its debtors.

The king agreed to the idea. He granted the trustees a 21-year **charter** to establish the colony. After 21 years Georgia would become a royal colony, which meant it would be run by the king.

The trustees paid the way to Georgia for debtors. They would also be given 50 acres (20 ha) of land. In return for this, the settlers would help build the colony. People who paid their own way would have 500 acres (202 ha).

Oglethorpe planned the layout of Savannah. He separated the land into squares. The streets around each square were lined with houses and community buildings. Farm animals were raised inside of the squares. Inset: Mary Musgrove spoke both English and the Creek language. She helped Oglethorpe and the Georgia settlers get along with the Creek people.

Settling Georgia

In November 1732, James Oglethorpe and 35 families set sail for Georgia. They landed on February 12, 1733. Oglethorpe found a Creek village on Yamacraw Bluff. He asked Tomochichi, a Creek chief, for permission to settle nearby. Tomochichi agreed, and the Creeks became friendly with the colonists.

The colonists called their settlement Savannah. Oglethorpe drew up a plan for the settlement. Next he built forts, including Fort Frederica, on Saint Simons Island, to secure the colony from the Spaniards who lived in Florida.

The trustees felt let down, however, because Oglethorpe did not get as many debtors to go to Georgia as they had hoped. To build the colony, Oglethorpe opened the settlement to people from other countries in 1734.

This picture shows the Spanish cutting off Robert Jenkins' ear, the act that began the war of the same name. Inset: Fort Frederica, on Georgia's Saint Simons Island, was the location of the Battle of Bloody Marsh in the War of Jenkins' Ear. The British win in the 1742 battle brought an end to the war.

Georgia's Early Years

The early Georgian settlers faced many troubles. During the colony's first year, many settlers died from illnesses. The colonists' crops also did not produce as much as they had expected. They then tried to grow different types of moneymaking crops. They found rice, indigo, and cotton worked well in Georgia's soil.

The colonists also faced attacks by the Spanish. In 1736, Oglethorpe asked King George II to send soldiers to the colony. The king refused because it would cost the government too much money. A few years later, the king sent troops to Georgia to fight the Spanish in the War of Jenkins' Ear.

In 1731, Spain arrested Robert Jenkins for illegally shipping goods to islands near Florida, which belonged to Spain. The Spanish cut off Jenkins' ear. Jenkins showed the ear to Parliament in Britain. The British went to war with Spain. The war became known as the War of Jenkins' Ear. The British beat the Spanish at the Battle of Bloody Marsh in 1742, and that ended the war.

In 1750, the Georgia Trustees ended the ban on slavery. With slave labor, colonists built large farms, called plantations. They grew rich growing crops such as rice, indigo, and cotton. This ended Oglethorpe's dream for the colony. Inset: In 1742, the Georgia Trustees printed this booklet. It explained why they did not allow colonists either to buy more land or to own slaves.

Slavery in Georgia

By 1740, many settlers wanted to leave Georgia and move to South Carolina. There people were getting rich by growing crops such as rice and cotton. South Carolina farmers were able to do this because they could buy huge farms, called plantations, and use slave labor.

To stop colonists from leaving Georgia, the trustees allowed them to rent more land. In 1750, the trustees lifted the ban on slavery. Soon more settlers moved to Georgia and built plantations. They began to use slave labor.

In 1752, the trustees turned Georgia over to King George II, and it became a royal colony. Royal colonies had a governor appointed by the king. They also had an elected **assembly**, whose members were chosen by the colony. Georgia's government was now like that of most of the other colonies.

Colonists were angry about the Stamp Act, and they found many ways to protest it. This picture shows colonists burning the hated stamps. Inset: This is one of the tax stamps printed for the unpopular Stamp Act in 1765.

Britain Taxes the Colonies

In 1754, Britain began the **French and Indian War** with France over land in North America. The British won the war in 1763, but then they needed to pay back the money they had borrowed to fight the war.

Since the war was fought in the colonies, Britain decided the colonists should pay for it through taxation. The British taxed the colonies on things such as sugar, glass, lead, silk cloth, and tea. The colonists had not been allowed to vote on these new taxes. In 1765, Britain passed the Stamp Act, which required the colonists to buy a stamp for every piece of paper that they used. These laws made the colonists angry. Some Georgians joined the **Sons of Liberty**, a group of colonists who **protested** against the Stamp Act. There were so many protests against the Stamp Act throughout the colonies that Britain did away with it in 1766.

As colonists turned away from Britain, those who stayed loyal were harmed in many ways. This picture shows a man being tarred and feathered for being a loyalist. Inset: This is a list of Georgian loyalists who had their land taken away from them. It is thought that about one-fifth of colonists were loyalists.

Georgia Remains Loyal to Britain

Georgians did not like being taxed, but they did not protest as much as northern colonists did. When the First Continental Congress met in Philadelphia, Pennsylvania, in 1774 to talk about their problems with Britain, Georgia did not send a **representative**.

At this time the colonists who wanted to be free from Britain were called patriots. Most Georgians, however, remained **loyal** to Britain. They were called loyalists. Georgia's loyalists felt this way for several reasons. Since Georgia had been a colony for only 40 years, many colonists still had strong ties to Britain. Georgia also depended on Britain for trade, because the colony sold many of its products to the British. As the call for independence grew in the colonies, Georgians would have to choose between remaining loyal to Britain or becoming part of a new nation.

From Georgia's State Constitution

"Whereas the conduct of the legislature of Great Britain for many years past has been so oppressive . . .

And whereas the independence of the United States of America has been also declared . . . and all political connection between them and the Crown of Great Britain is in consequence thereof dissolved:

We, therefore, the representatives of the people, from whom all power originates . . . do ordain and declare... the following rules and regulations be adopted for the future government of this State."

The opening statement of Georgia's constitution says that Britain's laws had become so unbearable that the colonies had to declare independence. As a result Georgia is creating its own government, which will represent its citizens.

This map from around 1775 shows the North American colonies and territories at the time of the American Revolution. Georgia is yellow on this map. Inset: Georgia's state constitution was printed in the Georgia Constitutional Gazette on March 31, 1777.

Georgia Declares Independence

The **American Revolution** began on April 19, 1775, when British soldiers and American patriots fought a battle in Lexington, Massachusetts. After the battle many people in Georgia sided with the patriots. One of Georgia's patriot leaders was Button Gwinnett.

After the war started, a group of Georgia's patriots stole the British supply of gunpowder in Savannah. They planned to use the gunpowder in battles against the British. Georgians sent food and money to the northern colonies to help them in their fight.

In May 1775, the Second Continental Congress met in Philadelphia. Its purpose was to **unite** the colonies and **declare** independence from Britain. Gwinnett represented Georgia at the Congress. The representatives wrote the **Declaration of Independence** in July 1776.

EXPLICATION DES LETTRES DU PLAN

A. Batterie de Gauche des Français de 6 Pièces de 11 et de 6 pièces de 12.
B. Batterie de Droite de 5 pièces de 11 et de 6 pièces de 11 à laquelle on a fait un retour pour 5 ... pour Opposer à la Batterie des Ennemis
C. Batterie des Français de 9 Mortiers du Calibre de 6 pouces jusqu'à celui de 9 p.
D. Batterie des Américains de quatre pièces de 4 placées Sur la Face gauche du Redon
E. Batterie des Ennemis d'Onze pièces de canon qu'ils ont Démasqués pendant le Siège
F. Batterie des Ennemis de 9 pièces de canon. (G. Batterie des ennemi de 5 pièces de Can
H. Batterie des Ennemis de 7 Mortiers. (I. Batt) des ennemis de 5 pièces de Can
K. Batterie ennemie à Gauche de la Redoute de Spring Hill de 5 pièces de Canon.
L. Batterie ennemie de 5 pièces de canon dont deux flanquent la Redoute de Spring
M. Batterie des ennemis de 5 pièces de Canon.
N. Batterie de 5 pièces de canon que les ennemis ont élevées pendant le Siège
O. Batt ennemie Sur la Rivière de 2 pièces de 12 qui tirait Sur la Flotte du Roy la Truitte et
P. Retranchement en Sable en Seconde ligne avec un Fossé large et Profond dans lequel la Savannah se trouvé à couvert du Feu des Assiégeans.
R. Batterie ennemie de 5 pièces au Bord de la Rivière à Gauche de la Ville
S. Place d'Arme en forme de Redoute (T) Magasin à Poudre
V. Corps de Cavalerie Démolis pendant le Siège.

NOTA

Les lignes ponctuées en Rouge en avant de la Redoute de Spring Hill Désignent la Marche que les Colonnes ont du Ou
les lignes ponctuées en Noir Désignent la Marche qu'elles ont Suivies Sur les lieux de l'Attaque.
le Débarquement des Français s'est fait dans un endroit nommé Bewlay à deux lieux dans la Rivière au
embarquèrent à 10 lieux au Sud de Savannah. il y a 5 lieux ½ de Bewlay à la Ville de Savannah Suivre elle même a 12
à Travers/bras de la R.Te Savannah. Théodore Français était Mouillées à 3 lieux au large de la Côte.
Du violent coup de Vent, et occasionné des avaries considérables à Bewlay, en rompant plusieurs fois sur la
troupes qu'elle avait à son lieu, et en faisant traverser celle celle en se formant levée de part/en tout qui résolurent...
Principaux Matelot qui ont emploie la Perte de Savannah et qui occasion dans les Operations un lenteur qui a laissé à l'Ennemi le tems de
...les Confédérales qu'elles ont disposées allègrés par le circonstance sur Siège ou en avant ont jamais deliré de Patrie.

Echelle de 1200 Toises ou d'½ Lieue de France

SIÈGE DE SAVANNAH
fait par les Troupes françoises aux Ordres du Général D'Estaing Vice-Amiral de France. en 7.bre et 8.bre 1779.

Savannah was occupied by the British from 1778, until the end of the Revolution. In the Battle of Savannah,, the patriots' Continental army, with help from the French, tried unsuccessfully to win the city back. This 1779 map shows the positions of the armies. Inset: Count Casimir Pulaski was killed in the Battle of Savannah.

The American Revolution in Georgia

The Continental army did not win many battles during the first years of the war. Few Georgians joined the army, because most of the battles took place far away in the northern colonies. Also many Georgians were loyalists.

In March 1776, the Battle of the Rice Boats was the first battle in Georgia. The British attacked Colonial ships in Savannah's harbor and stole the rice in the ships' hold. In 1778, the British returned to Savannah and occupied the city. Georgia remained occupied by the British until 1781, when the Continental army won at Yorktown, Virginia, and ended the fighting.

Count Casimir Pulaski was born in Poland in 1745. When he heard about the American Revolution, he wanted to help the colonists. In 1777, Pulaski was given command of the Continental army's cavalry. A cavalry is a group of soldiers who fight on horseback. Pulaski was killed in 1779, during the Battle of Savannah. A monument in Savannah honors Pulaski.

Georgia Joins the United States

The American Revolution officially ended when Britain and the new United States signed the Treaty of Paris in 1783. In 1787, leaders from the colonies formed the Constitutional Convention to decide on the type of government they wanted. They had been following the **Articles of Confederation** since 1781, but this set of laws was not working.

William Few and Abraham Baldwin represented Georgia at the convention. They wanted a strong central government and helped write the set of laws that became the **Constitution**, which the United States follows today. Few and Baldwin signed the Constitution for Georgia in September 1787. Georgia accepted the Constitution on January 2, 1788, and became the fourth state to join the United States.

Glossary

American Revolution (uh-MER-uh-ken reh-vuh-LOO-shun) Battles that soldiers from the colonies fought against Britain for freedom, from 1775 to 1783.

Articles of Confederation (AR-tih-kulz UV kun-feh-deh-RAY-shun) The laws that governed the United States before the Constitution was created.

assembly (uh-SEM-blee) A group of people who meet to advise a government.

charter (CHAR-tur) An official agreement giving someone permission to do something.

Constitution (kon-stih-TOO-shun) The basic rules by which the United States is governed.

debtors (DEH-turz) People who owe.

Declaration of Independence (deh-kluh-RAY-shun UV in-duh-PEN-dints) An official announcement signed on July 4, 1776, in which American colonists stated they were free of British rule.

declare (dih-KLAYR) To announce officially.

explorer (ek-SPLOR-ur) A person who travels and looks for new land.

French and Indian War (FRENCH AND IN-dee-un WOR) The battles fought between 1754 and 1763 by England, France, and Native Americans for control of North America.

loyal (LOY-ul) Faithful to a person or an idea.

protested (PROH-test-ed) Acted out in disagreement of something.

representative (reh-prih-ZEN-tuh-tiv) A person who speaks for another person or group of people.

Sons of Liberty (SUNZ UV LIH-ber-tee) A group of American colonists who were Whigs and who protested the British government's taxes and unfair treatment before the American Revolution.

unite (yoo-NYT) To bring together to act as a single group.

Index

Primary Sources

Page 4. *South-east Coast of America.* eighteenth century, Guillaume Raynal, published by Charles Marie Rigobert Bonne. **Page 6.** *A Rake's Progress VII: The Rake in Prison.* Oil on canvas, 1733, William Hogarth, Sir John Sloane's Museum, London. **Page 6. Inset.** Charter of Georgia. 1732, Georgia State Archives, Morrow, Georgia. **Page 10.** *A Spanish "Guarda Costa" (Coastguard) boarding Captain Jenkins's Ship and Cutting Off His Ear, 1731.* Engraving, eighteenth century. **Page 12. Inset.** *The Georgia Trustees Justify Their Policies.* 1742, Library of Congress, Washington, D.C. **Page 14. Inset.** *Stamp Issued in the Stamp Act.* Woodcut with watercolor wash, 1765. **Page 16. Inset.** *List of Loyalists Whose Lands Were Confiscated.* 1780s, Loyalist Papers, Georgia Historical Society, Savannah, Georgia. **Page 18. Inset.** Georgia State Constitution. Published in *Georgia Constitutional Gazette* March 31, 1777, Georgia Historical Society, Savannah, Georgia. **Page 20.** *Siege de Savannah.* 1779, Pierre Ozanne, Independence National Historical Park, Philadelphia.

Web Sites

Due to the changing nature of Internet links, PowerKids Press has developed an online list of Web sites related to the subject of this book. This site is updated regularly. Please use this link to access the list: www.powerkidslinks.com/lotc/georgia/